THE
FATAL FIRE

THE
FATAL FIRE

Illustrated by Helen Flook

A & C Black • London

www.acblack.com

Text copyright © 2008 Terry Deary
Illustrations copyright © 2008 Helen Flook

The rights of Terry Deary and Helen Flook to be identified as the
author and illustrator of this work have been asserted by them in
accordance with the Copyrights, Designs and Patents Act 1988.

ISBN 978-0-7136-8970-9

A CIP catalogue for this book is available from the British Library.

This book is produced using paper that is made from wood grown in
managed, sustainable forests. It is natural, renewable and recyclable.
The logging and manufacturing processes conform to the
environmental regulations of the country of origin.

Printed and bound in Great Britain by
CPI Cox & Wyman, Reading, RG1 8EX

ONE

Rome, AD 64

"Rome is a dangerous place, Mary," the old man whispered. He pulled a hood over his head to hide his face. "Death is all around us."

Mary looked about the street.
She could see lots of people... but
not this strange thing called Death.
"Where, master Tullus?" she
asked.

The shops in the street were closed. Today was the day of the chariot races. The shopkeepers knew that the crowds would pack the streets. And where there were crowds, there were thieves.

In all the shoving and shouting, the dust and the din, thieves would rob the shops and disappear quickly in the crush of the crowds.

Master Tullus pulled the girl into
a shop doorway. He leaned forward.
"See that man with one eye standing
on the corner?" he asked.

"Yes, master."

The girl could see the man with a
dark beard and a patch over one eye.

In the rushing rabble, he was the
one standing still on the corner.
His one eye flickered
round, watching
the scene.

"He's a thief,"
the old man
went on. "He's
waiting for a rich
man to pass by. If the
rich man is drunk then the one-eyed
villain will follow him. When the
crowd packs into the arena, he will
push up against the rich man. He'll
slip a hand into his toga and pinch
his purse!"

"He won't!"

"He will!"

"Shall we stop him?"

"He carries a knife. He'll cut your throat if you try. Would you like that?"

"No, master Tullus," the girl sighed. "How do you know this?"

"I've seen him hanging around the baths. When the men get undressed, he tries to creep into the changing room and search for their purses. Sometimes the slaves on guard get careless."

"He's a villain," Mary moaned.

"And he's not the worst. See those gangs?" her master asked.

"The ones carrying ribbons?" Mary had seen them, with their red or white, green or blue ribbons, charging down the street, bawling and battering people out of their way.

"The colours are the chariot team they support. They get very excited... some say they don't sleep the night before the races, and they drink a lot and can turn very nasty. The reds hate the whites and the blues hate the reds. *Everyone* hates the greens."

"Poor greens!"

"That's the emperor's team," the old man said.

"What colour are you?" Mary asked.

"Green, of course," her master smiled. "But don't tell that to a red, blue or white. They would probably give me a beating."

"Rome's a dangerous place," the girl groaned.

"I told you that before we left the house."

"You did, master Tullus," Mary nodded. This was the first time her master had let her go into the city with him. His serving boy was ill from eating a rotten snail, so she had to take his place.

Mary watched as the man with the eye patch slid into the rushing crowd, his eye on a fat man in a purple toga. And she shivered.

TWO

"If the thieves don't get you, the soldiers might," said master Tullus.

"Get me?" Mary squeaked. "Why?"

The old man's face was as wrinkled as a walnut shell, and it crinkled nastily as he said, "I know your secret, little Mary."

"Secret?"

"You're a cannibal!"

"I'm not!"

"You are one of those Christians, aren't you?"

"Yes, but..."

"And when you have your services, you eat bread and drink wine?"

"We do, but..."

"And you believe that the bread turns into the flesh of your god and the wine turns into his blood, don't you?"

"Well, yes..."

"So, you're cannibals. That's why you have to keep it secret. The people of Rome don't like you and your priests. They just need any excuse to turn on you and kill you all."

Mary's mouth was dry. She had heard about the executions. She didn't want to think about the horrors of the 'games', as the Romans called them. It wasn't much of a game being tied to a post while a bear tears off your flesh. She felt sick when a soldier walked past and gave her a hard glare.

The street became quieter, and the old man stepped out onto the path and followed the mob. In front of them stood a massive, wooden arena.

It had towering walls with dozens
of doors to let the noisy crowd in.

Street sellers had their stalls set up and were offering everything from food to clothes. Pans sizzled and steamed on small, wood-burning ovens.

"Sausages here! Get your sausages here!" came the cries.

"Thrushes, tasty thrushes!"

"Dormice, lovely stuffed dormice!"

"Slice of wild boar, sir? Killed fresh this morning!"

Mary's mouth was watering. Servants never got to eat much meat – they got by on thin porridge, some dates, onions and cheese.

The old man pointed to a sausage-seller's stall by one of the dark doorways. "Stay here till the games are finished."

"Here?"

"Here. You can't expect to come in and watch the chariot racing. It's not for the likes of you."

"But is it safe outside? With all the thieves and the soldiers?" Mary cried.

The old man pushed his crinkled face close to hers. "Who cares? You are a slave. A slave's life is worth nothing. You are a girl. A girl's life is worth nothing. So what are you worth?"

"Double nothing," Mary muttered and sank to the ground. Her master disappeared into the arena. Then she crawled under the stall to escape the heat of the midday sun.

THREE

In time, the street became empty and the food-sellers' cries stopped. Everyone was inside the arena and the roar of the crowd told Mary that the races had begun. Even the street sellers had deserted their stalls to watch.

Mary collected two ants from
the dusty earth and set them to run.
She would have her own races to
keep herself amused.

One ant raced out from under the
stall and into the sunlit street. Mary
lifted the cloth a little and that's
when she saw a pair of feet walking
past. And she knew at once that
all the dangers of Rome were just a
cubit away from her frightened face.

There was something wicked about those dusty feet in the dustier sandals. The crowd in the arena was roaring like a thousand lions, yet the feet seemed to be trying to walk on tiptoe. They took two steps and stopped. The ankles twisted as if the owner of the feet was looking around. Then they moved on, silent and snake-like.

Mary pulled the cloth back further and blinked out into the glare of the street. The feet rose into hairy legs and the legs went into a tunic with a green belt. But the man was too tall for her to see his face... unless she pushed her head right out.

"I'm not doing that," she thought. "My life's worth double nothing – but it's the only one I've got."

Again the man twisted to look around. Then he leaned forwards and took a sausage pan from the top of the stove. He threw the fat from the pan onto the wooden wall of the arena.

Then he took a wooden spoon, opened the stove door and scooped hot ashes into the pan. The hot ashes set the remaining fat alight.

The man seemed to panic. He threw the burning mess at the wall and at once the sausage fat started to blaze.

The sandals began to run back towards the city and Mary could see the man's back now. She stuck her head out from the stall to see more clearly. The man stopped at the corner and turned. The serving girl saw the beard and the eye patch, and she gasped.

The thief did a curious thing —
he lifted the patch from his eye
to get a better look at the arena.
Then he gave a cruel grin and
hurried out of sight.

Mary tumbled out from under the
stall. She snatched the cloth from the
table and beat at the flames that were
steadily climbing the arena wall.

But the fat was burning fiercely and she only managed to set fire to the cloth, which scorched her hand. She dropped the cloth and watched in horror as the greasy sausage table burst into flames.

FOUR

Mary looked around for water. There was none. She threw herself into the arena entrance. She ran inside and up some steps that led out into the rows of seats.

Luckily, the first race had finished so the crowd had quietened down. Hundreds of people were able to hear her scream:

"Fire – the arena's on fire!"

The masses turned and saw the smoke rising.

The arena was huge and there were lots of ways to escape. In the time it takes for a chariot race, the place was empty and the frightened horses had been led away.

Mary followed the crowd that hurried through the streets. She looked back to see the arena was already a wall of flame.

There hadn't been any rain for weeks, and the blue, spark-spangled smoke rose into a clear sky. A breeze blew the smoke towards the city and showers of fiery soot fell on the houses and temples.

The cloud of smoke travelled faster than Mary could run. By the time she'd reached the centre of the city, some of the roofs were already smoking and people were running to save their families and their homes. A few tried to gather buckets and form a chain from the fountain.

But the fire from the sky was defeating them.

Mary sprinted to her master's house and panted her message: "Rome is burning!"

The servants ran to the pond in the garden and plunged in a bundle of blankets. They threw them onto the roof to stop it catching alight.

Master Tullus hobbled in to give orders. "Load a cart with our best gold and silver ornaments. Take them out to my country villa. If this house burns, it burns. The gods will have their way."

Mary helped load small statues that were studded with precious stones. Then she ran behind the cart towards the hills.

When at last the family and
servants were safely away from the
thundering roar of falling buildings,
they looked back. Everything in the
path of the breeze was burning. Half
of Rome was tumbling into ruin.

"All from one sausage pan," Mary groaned.

"What was that?" her master snapped.

"Nothing, master. Nothing," she said and turned to follow the cart. She muttered a prayer to her god. "He saw me, didn't he? The man with the eye patch... Just before he disappeared, he saw me. He knows I saw him. He'll try to find me and kill me, won't he? You will look after me, won't you?"

Mary's god didn't answer.

FIVE

Rome lay in ruins. It smelled of smoke and soot. Mary led the donkey that carried master Tullus back into the city.

The old man couldn't stop chuckling. "Oh, Mary, today could be the day that sees more excitement than a hundred chariot races."

"Yes, master Tullus," she said, and shook her foot to get rid of a stone that had stuck in her sandal.

"Don't you want to know *why* it will be exciting?" he cackled.

"Yes, master," she said wearily.

"Because today could be the last day of the emperor Nero. He could be thrown out of Rome... or even killed! And it will serve him right. He is a cruel man... of course I can't *say* that he is cruel or he'd have me executed in some horrible new way."

"But you *did* say it, master," Mary pointed out.

"Ah, but only to you... and you don't matter."

"No, master." Mary led the way through the city gates and passed a group of weeping people who were searching the warm ruins for anything they could rescue.

"The tales they tell about Nero! He had his own mother murdered, you know? Then he had his wife murdered so he could marry the lovely Poppea. And what did he do to Poppea?"

"I don't know, master."

"He kicked her to death! Then he ordered his teacher, Seneca, to kill himself. Poor old fellow had to do it, too. But this time Nero's gone too far. Do you know what he's done?"

"No, master."

"He started the fire that burned down Rome."

Mary stumbled and almost fell under the hooves of the donkey.

"No, he didn't!" she cried.

"Don't argue with me, girl, or I'll have you whipped till the skin is peeled off your back!" spat master Tullus. "Now, help me down. We are at the senate."

"The what?"

"The senate – the place where the great men of Rome meet. The emperor will be here to answer some tough questions!"

Mary stopped the donkey in front of a shining building of marble columns and soaring roofs. The fire had not touched it. She helped master Tullus fold his toga neatly and watched him enter the building along with other fine gentlemen.

Men and women were gathering outside the senate looking angry. They were muttering among themselves. When one man cried out, "It's all Nero's fault!" a troop of soldiers moved in to arrest him.

The man was led away screaming. The rest of the mob fell silent.

The scowling rabble scared Mary. She had to wait for her master, but not here, she thought. Then she did something that would save her life... She followed her master into the senate.

SIX

The large marble hall was packed with men and servants and no one noticed Mary as she slipped into a corner.

The voices inside were as loud
and angry as the ones outside.
She heard the words "Nero" and
"fire" and "palace" spoken a lot
in vicious voices.

Suddenly there was a trumpet
blast and the men fell silent.
Someone cried, "My Lords, we
have the honour of greeting
Nero, emperor of Rome!"

Everyone turned towards a platform at the end of the hall. Mary was too small to see through the thick wall of togas, but she could hear.

"Gentlemen! Greetings from your emperor," came a whining voice.

That must be Nero, she thought.

"I have heard the foolish stories," he sighed. "They are nonsense."

"Emperor," someone shouted, and Mary knew it was the voice of master Tullus. "The people are saying you had your servants start the fire."

"I swear by almighty Jupiter that is not true," the emperor laughed.

"You came here a year ago and asked us to knock down many streets to build a new palace," master Tullus went on.

"A golden palace that will be the wonder of the world. It will bring glory to Rome," Nero added.

"We refused to let you knock down the streets..."

"But now they've burned down!" Nero giggled madly. "The golden palace can be built!"

"But..." master Tullus began.

"I know! People think that is why I started the fire. But I am here to tell you two things. First, I was in my summer house over in Antium when the fire started – ask my servants! And second, I have spies in the city of Rome, and I know who *really* started the fire!"

Every lord in the senate seemed to gasp at the news. At last master Tullus cried, "So who was it, Emperor?"

SEVEN

Nero's eyes opened wide as if he were afraid of what he was about to say. He licked his greasy lips and began to speak quickly.

"There is a dangerous little group of people who are getting stronger all the time. They want to destroy our palaces and our temples. They want to kill the great Jupiter and all our gods. They are cannibals! They eat flesh and they will happily burn down Rome to ruin us all. They are called Christians, my friends. We must seek them out and destroy them! Every last one. They will be placed on poles and covered in tar, then set alight. They will burn like torches to light up Rome and show the world what we do to rebels. They will be torn apart in the games – I will build a new arena when I build my golden house! They will be crucified by the road

sides and they will be stoned in
the streets. They shall never defeat
Nero and his Roman heroes."
The emperor was screaming now
and the lords were starting to cheer
his words. "Go out there and find
these snakes, these fire raisers,
these devils! Kill them all!"

The lords stepped back to let the raging Nero leave.

Mary crept towards the door but the crowd of men in togas blocked her path. Mary found herself looking through a gap between two togas just as the emperor marched past. He had no beard now, but she knew his face.

The last time she had seen it, he had been wearing an eye patch. The last time she had seen him, he had been running from the fire he had started.

Now it was Mary's turn to run. First to warn the Christian leaders, Peter and Paul, before the hunt started. And then to try and save herself.

Mary ran and the words of master Tullus came back to her.

"Rome is a dangerous place, Mary," the old man had whispered. "A dangerous place..."

She ran as if the Devil himself was after her... She remembered the cruel face of the emperor... Maybe he was.

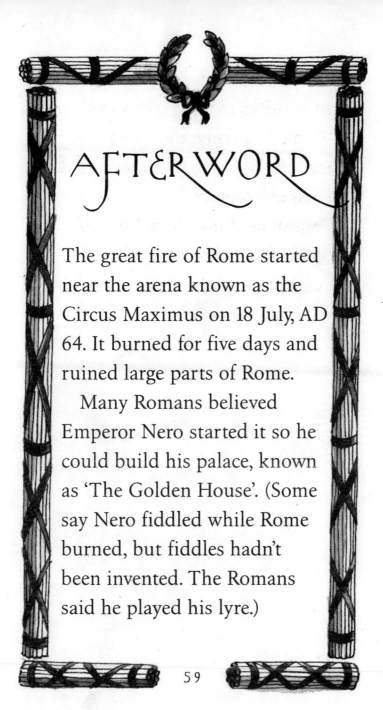

AFTERWORD

The great fire of Rome started near the arena known as the Circus Maximus on 18 July, AD 64. It burned for five days and ruined large parts of Rome.

Many Romans believed Emperor Nero started it so he could build his palace, known as 'The Golden House'. (Some say Nero fiddled while Rome burned, but fiddles hadn't been invented. The Romans said he played his lyre.)

Nero blamed the Christians for the fire. For the next 300 years they were hunted down and killed in dozens of cruel ways. The Romans soon captured the Christian leaders, Saint Peter and Saint Paul, who were probably in Rome at the time of the fire, and executed them. But the Christian religion just grew stronger, and lasted far longer than the Roman Empire.

Nero got his Golden House ... but by AD 68 the Romans were tired of Nero's cruelty. He was driven from Rome and

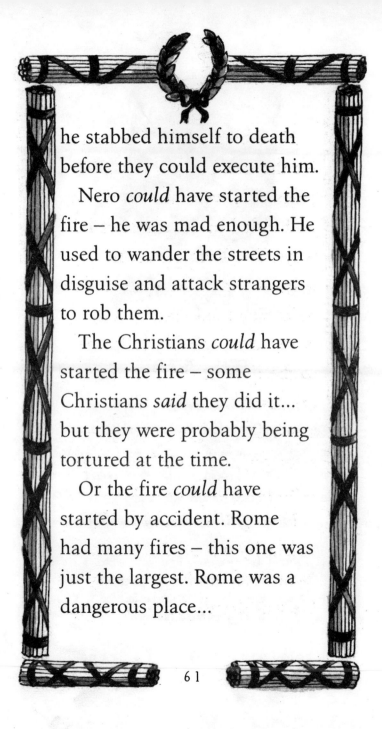

he stabbed himself to death before they could execute him.

Nero *could* have started the fire – he was mad enough. He used to wander the streets in disguise and attack strangers to rob them.

The Christians *could* have started the fire – some Christians *said* they did it... but they were probably being tortured at the time.

Or the fire *could* have started by accident. Rome had many fires – this one was just the largest. Rome was a dangerous place...

ROME, 387 BC

The cruel Gauls are attacking Rome.
High on the Capitol Hill, the priests have been
defending the temple of Juno for weeks. But food
is running out and their only hope of help is from
the army of Lord Furius. Will he arrive in time?
And what will they do if he doesn't?

Roman Tales are exciting, funny stories based
on historical events - short chapters and
illustrations throughout are perfect for
building reading confidence.

ISBN 978 0 7136 8963 1   £4.99

ROME, AD 51

Deri is in prison. The outspoken Celt was
heard criticising Rome and now faces execution
in the morning. Luckily, his cell mate Caratacus is
a very special prisoner indeed - a British chief.
He believes there is a way to save both their
skins, but first he will need Deri's help.

Roman Tales are exciting, funny stories based
on historical events - short chapters and
illustrations throughout are perfect for
building reading confidence.

ISBN 978 0 7136 8960 0   £4.99

ROME, AD 113

Pertinax is helping prepare magnificent
dishes for a feast to be held by the great
lawyer Pliny. While the boy is working,
Pliny tells him the story of a terrifying ghost
who haunted a garden not unlike Pliny's own.
But there's no truth in ghost stories... is there?

Roman Tales are exciting, funny stories based
on historical events - short chapters and
illustrations throughout are perfect for
building reading confidence.

ISBN 978 0 7136 8961 7   £4.99